BREAKFAST
WITH MY FATHER

BREAKFAST WITH MY FATHER

by Ron Roy
pictures by
Troy Howell

 Houghton Mifflin/Clarion Books/New York

For Jim Giblin, my friend and editor, with gratitude.

Houghton Mifflin/Clarion Books
52 Vanderbilt Avenue, New York, NY 10017

Text copyright © 1980 by Ron Roy
Illustrations copyright © 1980 by Troy Howell

Library of Congress Cataloging in Publication Data

Roy, Ronald, 1940-   Breakfast with my father.
Summary: After his parents separate, David looks forward to outings with his father and wonders what has happened when he doesn't arrive at Frank's Diner for their customary Saturday breakfast.
[1. Fathers and sons—Fiction] I. Howell, Troy. II. Title.
PZ7.R8139Br   [E]   80-12963   ISBN 0-395-29430-4

When David's father moved out of the house, David
thought he would never see him again.

But early the next Saturday morning he came to David's room and sat on his bed. He put his hand gently on the side of David's face until David woke up.

"Hi, Davey."

"Dad! What are you doing here?"

"I came to take my kid to breakfast. Get dressed, and don't wake the baby."

"Isn't Mom coming too?" David asked.

"No," his father said softly.

"Why not?"

"Mom and I aren't going to be seeing each other for a while," his father said.

"Are you getting a divorce?" David asked.

"No, Davey, we're just separated for now."

"For how long?"

David's father tickled him. "Don't ask so many questions," he said. "Let's go eat."

So they did, every Saturday that winter.

First David would get dressed in the dark.
Then he would tiptoe past the baby's room and tiptoe
past his mother's room.

He would climb into the car and his father would drive
to Frank's Diner.

Inside Frank's it was warm and smelled like coffee.

Frank always took their order himself. "What'll it be, men?"

David's father would say, "Fried chicken eggs and coffee, please."

David would say, "Cheerios and orange juice, please."

Then Frank would slap down the silverware and go off toward the kitchen.

"Why do you order chicken eggs?" David asked one Saturday morning.

"Because they're all out of dinosaur eggs," his father answered.

Frank always smiled when he brought their food. "Here you are, men."

David's father would wink at David over his coffee cup.
David would wink back over his juice.

When it was time to leave, David's father always let him pay. Sometimes David got to keep the change for his allowance.

Then they would drive back to David's house. David's father would hug him. "See you next week, sport. Take care of Mommy and the baby."

It was the same every Saturday morning.

Then one Saturday, when winter was over, David's father did not come to his room.

He did not sit on David's bed.

He did not put his hand gently on David's face.

David woke up by himself. But he stayed in bed. And he kept his eyes shut tight just in case his father came.

But he didn't.

David heard his mother come to give the baby her bottle.

He heard some squirrels arguing over nuts outside his window.

Everyone is having breakfast except me, David thought.

Then David heard a noise in the hall. He pretended to be asleep.

His door opened and he heard footsteps. Someone sat on his bed. A warm hand touched his face.

"David? Are you awake?"

It was his mother.

"No," David said.

"Are you getting up for breakfast?"

"No."

"Please come, I've made sausages and pancakes."

"NO!" David pulled the blankets over his head.

But when his mother left he stuck his nose out of the covers.
He thought about his father who hadn't come.
He thought about the sausages in the kitchen.

I'll go, but I won't eat, David decided.
He put on his robe and slippers and walked downstairs.

He could smell the sausages. I'll eat just one, he thought.

When he got to the kitchen he stared.

The baby was in her high chair putting cereal in her hair.

His mother was mixing something at the sink.

His father was drinking coffee at the table.

"Hi, Davey," his father said.

"Dad! What are you doing here?"

"I'm having breakfast with my family."

"How long are you staying?" David asked.

David's father looked at his mother.
"Today and tomorrow," he said. "Then we'll see."

"Are you two going to gab all morning?" his mother asked. "I'm starving!"

David piled three pancakes on his plate.

His father winked at him over his coffee.

David winked back over his orange juice.